Missile Toe
A Very Confused Christmas

Colin—
BE MERRY!

Marty Kelley

Written by Devin Scillian & Illustrated by Marty Kelley

I know Jesus and Santa and Rudolph's nose.
I know about Frosty when he came unfroze.

I know Dasher and Dancer, Comet and Cupid.
But sometimes I feel like I'm Christmas stupid....

Deck the Halls

The song says I should "deck the halls,"

But I don't know what to do.

Where are these halls? What kind of deck?

I haven't got a clue.

Do they mean a deck of cards?

Like Go Fish or some other game?

The hall that leads to the bathroom?

Or is it the Hall of Fame?

Yes, I'd like to deck the halls,
But I'm failing this Christmas quiz.
I'm supposed to do it with Holly.
And I don't know where she is.

Sugarplums

I'm making out my Christmas list, and I hope when Santa comes
This will be the year at last I get some sugarplums.
Every year I write it down in letters big and red.
"**SUGARPLUMS!**" just like the ones dancing in my head.

What are those things? I have to know. Oh, they sound so yummy.
I've got to have some sugarplums dancing in my tummy.

Are they crunchy or gooey? Creamy or tart?
Big? Or dainty and little?
Do they last all day? Can two people share?
Is there a great big seed in the middle?

My list this year is one item long. Santa will know who it's from.
I'd trade it all if I could have just one little sugarplum.

Johnny Oats Ate Nicholas

Johnny Oats ate Nicholas,
Our dear departed guppy.
We weren't happy with Johnny Oats,
But I said, "He's just a puppy!"
"I guess that's true," my mother sighed,
And I thought that was that.
But two days later Johnny belched,
And we couldn't find the cat.
Earl the parrot, Clark the snake,
The guinea pigs, Pooh and Tigger.
One by one, our pets disappeared,
And Johnny Oats got bigger.
We took Johnny Oats to see the vet.
It was a problem; we couldn't deny it.
"We love this dog," my mother said,
"But we're concerned about his diet."
"Let's have a look," the doctor said,
Leaning in for a better view.
And Johnny Oats opened wide
And tried to eat the doctor, too!
"You'll ruin your dinner," my mother laughed.
"Oh, he loves to chew!"

The doctor sighed and said to us,
"I know just what to do.
Bad dog! Bad dog!" the doctor yelled.
Which we found rather stern.
But the doc said, "Puppies need a guiding hand,
Or else they never learn."
The holes in the carpet, the missing shoes,
The curtains he'd torn up.
Maybe the problem with Johnny Oats
Was the way we were raising our pup.
So life's much better with Johnny Oats.
He's been much slower to grow.
'Cause cute little puppies will eat anything
Until you tell them "**NO!**"

Beth the Ham

Our Christmas play is quite a mess.
We're in a Christmas jam.
The sets are nice, the costumes, too.
The problem is Beth the ham.

She's not playing Mary; she's not an angel.
She's a sheep, for crying out loud.
But she just keeps breaking into song,
Hamming it up for the crowd.

She tells a few jokes; she juggles some fruit.
She brings her own spotlight.
She dances a tap number and does the splits
At the end of "O, Holy Night."

The Bible never mentions
An obnoxious little lamb.
Our Christmas play is just a mess
Thanks to Beth the ham.

The Wee Three Kings of Orientar

The Wee Three Kings of Orientar
Had crowns jeweled and shiny
That constantly slipped down over their ears,
For their heads were impossibly tiny.

They sat on thrones the size of a thimble,
Like three little royal elves,
And they never accomplished a single thing.
They just bickered among themselves.

"I'm the biggest!" the first would say.
"I'm bigger than you by far!"
"That's a lie!" the second would yell.
"I'm twice as big as you are!"

"You're a shrimp!" hollered the third.
"And you? You're just a tyke!"
But the castle cat decided all three
Tasted exactly alike.

The Ghost of Christmas Presents

All of the kids are running downstairs. They won't listen to me.
But the Ghost of Christmas Presents might be near the tree.

I heard about it in a movie, and there's a book about it, too.
You open up your Christmas gifts, and a scary voice says, "**BOO!**"

I don't care what Santa left. Tomorrow is soon enough.
I don't need some Christmas ghost hanging around my stuff.

Wild Shepherds Washed Their Flocks by Night

Wild shepherds washed their flocks by night,
And that was the start of their troubles.
As midnight came, the sheep ran away,
Completely covered in bubbles.

The trouble with wool is drying it right,
As any good label advises.
Those sheep looked silly when they finally came back.
Their sweaters had shrunk three sizes.

So they washed them again and they stretched and they pulled
And the sheep were terribly grumpy.
But finally the sheep were the proper size
Though they all looked a little bit lumpy.

So tend to your flock but always make sure
You bathe your sheep in the light.
There's nothing but trouble waiting for shepherds
Who wash their flocks by night.

O, Holey Knight

Oh, holey Knight, what's happened to you?
Your chest has a hole and your shoulder has two.

Four holes in your stomach, and three in your heart.
Oh, holey Knight, you're falling apart!

I can see through your tummy and you're missing both knees.
Good Sir Knight, you're a piece of Swiss cheese!

Retire right now and go be a farmer.
Or at least start wearing a good set of armor.

Round John Verjun

Silent night, holy night.
All is calm, all is bright.

Joseph says, "The man by the door?
I don't think I've seen him before."

He's just a guy, jolly and round,
Standing and smiling, not making a sound.

Joseph leans in. "How do you do?
I hate to be rude, but who are you?"

"I'm round John Verjun," he says with a grin.
"I saw the light on. I let myself in.

"Congratulations. Your baby is sweet.
I'm a little hungry. Is there something to eat?"

"So it's kings and shepherds," Joseph smiled.
"Round John Verjun, Mother, and child."

Angels We Half Heard on High

Angels we half heard on high, mumbling something in the sky.
"What's that?" we yelled, but they flew on by,
Those angels we half heard on high.

SNO-TÜB

Missile Toe

Missile Toe the soccer star
Could kick it high and kick it far.
Every kick was just the same,
But Missile Toe had lousy aim.
And we never won a single game.

Til yesterday. It was a scoreless tie.
"Today's the day!" came our battle cry.
Our goalie punted; it came to me.
I sent it on with a well-timed knee,
And Missile Toe was racing free.

Missile Toe gave the goal a glance.
He'd never have a better chance.
Their goalie was down, leaving a gap.
We knew he'd give that ball a slap,
But this one time, it was just…
…a
…tap.

We cheered as it rolled inside the post.
And Missile Toe cheered the most.
He jumped up high, his face aglow.
We cheered and sang down below,
And we hugged and kissed beneath Missile Toe.

I'll Be a Gnome for Christmas

I'll be a gnome for Christmas.

And you can be an elf.

And we'll live in the little Christmas house

That sits on Grandma's shelf.

We'll share the crumbs of a Christmas cookie,

And the bits of a candy cane.

And leave the prints of our tiny hands

On the frosty windowpane.

We'll take ourselves for a little walk
Through the boughs of the Christmas tree,
And then settle down inside a stocking,
As snug as we can be.

We'll keep one eye on the tiny plate
Of goodies that we'll leave,
And maybe, just maybe, we'll get a glimpse
Of Santa Christmas Eve.

For Theo and Roxy, with love.
–Devin

·

For Dave, Katie, Jacob, Matthew, and Sydney.
We always have a good time at our fun, old-fashioned family Christmases!

–Marty

Sleeping Bear Press˘
2395 South Huron Parkway, Suite 200
Ann Arbor, MI 48104
www.sleepingbearpress.com

Printed and bound in China.

10 9 8 7 6 5 4 3 2 1

Library of Congress Cataloging-in-Publication Data

Names: Scillian, Devin, author. | Kelley, Marty, illustrator.
Title: Missile toe : a very confused Christmas / written by Devin Scillian ;
illustrated by Marty Kelley.
Description: Ann Arbor, MI : Sleeping Bear Press, [2017] | Audience: 4–8.
Identifiers: LCCN 2017006280 | ISBN 9781585363711 (hardcover)
Subjects: LCSH: Children's poetry, American. | Christmas poetry.
Classification: LCC PS3619.C55 A6 2017 | DDC 811/.6—dc23
LC record available at https://lccn.loc.gov/2017006280